THIS BOOK

BELONGS TO:

....

....

THE STORY OF
*A Fierce Bad
Rabbit*

THE STORY OF
A FIERCE BAD RABBIT

BY

BEATRIX POTTER

A PETER RABBIT™

110th Anniversary Edition

FREDERICK WARNE

FREDERICK WARNE

Published by the Penguin Group
Penguin Books Ltd., 80 Strand, London WC2R 0RL, England
Penguin Group (USA) Inc., 375 Hudson Street, New York, New York 10014, USA
Penguin Group (Australia), 250 Camberwell Road, Camberwell,
Victoria 3124, Australia (a division of Pearson Australia Group Pty. Ltd.)
Penguin Group (Canada), 90 Eglinton Avenue East, Suite 700, Toronto,
Ontario M4P 2Y3, Canada (a division of Pearson Penguin Canada Inc.)
Penguin Books India Pvt. Ltd., 11 Community Centre, Panchsheel Park, New Delhi—110 017, India
Penguin Group (NZ), 67 Apollo Drive, Rosedale, Auckland 0632,
New Zealand (a division of Pearson New Zealand Ltd.)
Penguin Books (South Africa) (Pty.) Ltd, 24 Sturdee Avenue, Rosebank, Johannesburg 2196, South Africa

Penguin Books Ltd., Registered Offices: 80 Strand, London WC2R 0RL, England

Website: www.peterrabbit.com

First published by Frederick Warne in 1906
First published with reset text and new reproductions
of Beatrix Potter's illustrations in 2002
This edition published in 2011

003 - 10 9 8 7 6 5 4 3

New reproductions copyright © Frederick Warne & Co., 2002
Original copyright in text and illustrations © Frederick Warne & Co., 1906
Frederick Warne & Co. is the owner of all rights, copyrights and trademarks
in the Beatrix Potter character names and illustrations.

Colour reproduction by
EAE Creative Colour Ltd, Norwich
Printed and bound in China

PUBLISHER'S NOTE

The Story of A Fierce Bad Rabbit was originally inspired by a comment from Louie Warne, the daughter of Beatrix's publisher Harold Warne. She complained that Peter Rabbit was too well-behaved, and she wanted a story about a *really* naughty bunny!

Beatrix obliged with this simple tale, which was originally intended as one of the 1906 series of three concertina books, a format Frederick Warne & Co. had devised for very young children. Unfortunately the books fared badly in shops, where customers unfolded them and then damaged them in awkward attempts to get them back into their envelopes. In 1916, the two existing titles, *The Story of A Fierce Bad Rabbit* and *The Story of Miss Moppet* were reformatted as conventional books.

THIS IS A FIERCE BAD RABBIT; look at his savage whiskers, and his claws and his turned-up tail.

THIS is a nice gentle Rabbit. His mother has given him a carrot.

THE bad Rabbit would like some carrot.

HE doesn't say "Please." He takes it!

AND he scratches the good
Rabbit very badly.

THE good Rabbit creeps away,
and hides in a hole. It feels sad.

THIS is a man with a gun.

HE sees something sitting on a bench. He thinks it is a very funny bird!

HE comes creeping up behind
the trees.

AND then he shoots — BANG!

THIS is what happens—

BUT this is all he finds on the bench, when he rushes up with his gun.

THE good Rabbit peeps out of
its hole,

AND it sees the bad Rabbit tearing past — without any tail or whiskers!

THE END